THE DINO FILES

A Mysterious Egg

Stacy McAnulty

illustrations by **Mike Boldt**

A STEPPING STONE BOOK™
Random House 🏠 New York

For Henry

Text copyright © 2016 by Stacy McAnulty
Cover art and interior illustrations copyright © 2016 by Mike Boldt

Visit us on the Web!
SteppingStonesBooks.com
randomhousekids.com

Educators and librarians, for a variety of teaching tools, visit us at
RHTeachersLibrarians.com

Library of Congress Cataloging-in-Publication Data
McAnulty, Stacy.
A mysterious egg / Stacy McAnulty ; illustrated by Mike Boldt.
p. cm. — (The dino files ; # 1)
"A Stepping Stone Book."
Summary: During a summer at his grandparents' dinosaur museum and dig, the Dinosaur Education Center of Wyoming, Frank, aided by his cousin Sam and cat Saurus, cares for a newly hatched dinosaur while trying to keep its existence secret, both from his grandparents and from the neighbors.
ISBN 978-0-553-52191-7 (trade) — ISBN 978-0-553-52192-4 (lib. bdg.) —
ISBN 978-0-553-52193-1 (ebook)
[1. Dinosaurs—Fiction. 2. Animals—Infancy—Fiction. 3. Cousins—Fiction. 4. Paleontology—Fiction.] I. Boldt, Mike, illustrator. II. Title.
PZ7.M47825255My 2016 [Fic]—dc23 2014047419

Printed in the United States of America
10 9 8 7 6 5 4 3 2 1

This book has been officially leveled by using the
F&P Text Level Gradient™ Leveling System.

Random House Children's Books supports the
First Amendment and celebrates the right to read.

CONTENTS

Dear Reader,

You have this book because I know I can trust you. But just to be sure, I need you to take this oath. Please raise your right hand and say:

I, (now say your name), promise not to tell anyone about the story written on these pages. Never ever! I will keep everything that I learn locked tight in my brain and I'll throw away the key. If I do spill Frank Mudd's secrets, may I grow a horn on my nose and a tail from my butt.

Thank you for your loyalty.

Sincerely,
Frank Mudd
Future Paleontologist*
(That's a dinosaur scientist.)

P.S. If you do tell anyone my secrets, I'll say that I made it all up. I'll say it's fiction. (But believe me, it's not.)

* All the big dinosaur-like words are explained in my glossary.

I know books usually have the About the Author in the back (and it's usually really boring). But since this book is about me and my secret, I'm putting it in the front . . . plus I'm definitely not boring.

The author of this epic book is Frank L. Mudd. He's nine years old, handsome, and a dinosaur expert. He lives in North Carolina with his mom, his dad, and his cat. His favorite food is dessert. His favorite sport is Frisbee. His favorite subject is science. His favorite season is summer because he spends it in Wyoming. Frank's kind of bad at math, spelling, cursive, Frisbee, dancing, bird calls, and flipping pancakes.

Frank L. Mudd Dino Expert

This picture will probably be in a museum someday.

Welcome to DECoW

My grandparents own the Dinosaur Education Center of Wyoming. We call it DECoW. And it's the best place on the planet. Mom, Dad, and I visit on holidays, but during summer vacation I get to come by myself.

DECoW has a museum with a lab and seven dig sites. The dig sites are the most awesome because scientists and visitors (and me) can hunt for dinosaur fossils.

I'm really good at finding fossils. Yesterday I found a hadrosaurid tooth.

But Gram won't let me in the field today because I've got a sunburn. I just know they're about to make a huge, HUGE discovery. I can feel it in my stomach. Also, when Gram left the house, she said, "It's going to be a big day."

I need to be at that dig site!

Instead, I'm stuck inside the museum with PopPop. The good thing is I got my own name tag. Finally.

I was really hoping for PRESIDENT or just plain BOSS. PopPop calls me his best worker. But I'm not a real worker because I don't even get paid. Except sometimes PopPop buys me a soda from the vending machine when I do a good job.

"Can I please go to the dig site? Please?" I ask. Politely. Again.

"Why don't you do the ten a.m. sweep?" PopPop says.

He doesn't mean sweep with a broom. Every hour we walk through the museum and make sure everything is a-okay.

"Fine." I take the job and bring my cat, Saurus, with me. She's super lazy, so I push her through the museum in her catmobile. It's really just an old stroller, but don't tell Saurus that.

The museum is a giant loop that starts about 4 billion years ago in the Hadean Eon, when the earth was born. This isn't very exciting, and most visitors walk really fast through this part. (No running is allowed in the museum.) Actually, they ignore just about everything until they get to the Mesozoic Era (about 250 million years ago). Dinosaurs!

"Looking good, boys and girls," I say as Saurus and I check on the fossils.

A lady and her two kids stare at me.

I point to my name tag. "It's okay. I work here."

I straighten a PLEASE DO NOT TOUCH sign in front of the *Microraptors.* Then I pick up a candy wrapper.

"Big Bob, were you eating in here?" I ask our largest, awesomest fossil. (There's no eating allowed in the museum.) Big Bob is the most complete *Supersaurus* in the world. He's a celebrity. The fossil was discovered about a mile from here when my dad was a boy.

Saurus meows from her catmobile. She doesn't

like dinosaurs as much as I do. She likes naps and smelly canned food.

I wave goodbye to Big Bob. Then we walk by the *Triceratops* and *Spinosaurus.* When we get to the *T. rex,* my eyes almost pop out of my head. There are footprints in the sand under the fossil. The footprints are human. Sneakers, to be exact. And I know who made them!

"Samantha McCarthy, I know you're in there!" I yell.

"Roooooooar!" She jumps out from behind a fake tree.

"Get down!"

But instead of getting down, she holds a plastic microphone to her mouth. "I just scared my cousin Frank. He's afraid of almost everything. Dark places. Fireworks. Girls." She always pretends to talk to an invisible camera. She says she has to practice being famous.

"You aren't supposed to be on the displays.

You could break something." (There's no climbing allowed in the museum.)

"I'm not going to break anything." Sam swings from the *T. rex*'s rib. "Come up here. It's fun." She's three weeks older than me, but she doesn't act like it.

I've been staying with Gram and PopPop every summer since kindergarten. For some reason (that only makes sense to the grown-ups), my mom and Aunt Sophie thought it would be a good idea if Sam came to stay this summer too. Sam doesn't even like dinosaurs. I don't know what she likes, besides getting in trouble, her microphone, and bragging.

"Leave me alone. I'm working." I walk away with the catmobile. Sam follows without being invited. She doesn't even have a name tag.

"Don't you want to do something fun?" She holds the microphone in my face. "We can practice soccer."

"I'm busy, Sam." I push the microphone away.

For some reason (that only makes sense to the grown-ups), my grandparents signed us up to play soccer this summer. Sam and I are on the same team. I don't hate soccer. I would just rather be studying fossils than kicking a ball.

"Do you want to look for scorpions under the rocks in the parking lot?" Sam asks.

"No."

"Do you want to make a music video? I have a camera. A real one." Sam lives near Hollywood, California. She was on TV once when she was a baby. So she thinks she's famous.

"I said I'm working."

Saurus and I finish our sweep. Sam is still behind us. I take out the feather duster.

"It's fine by me if you kids want to play," PopPop says. "I can handle the register."

"Can we go to the dig site?" I ask.

"No," PopPop says.

"Then I want to work here," I say.

"This place is so boring." Sam plops down on a stool.

Just then, the front door opens. I hope Sam remembers to smile and be friendly. She's not good at that. But it's not a customer. It's Gram.

"Frank, Sam, you have to come see this." Gram's face is red and shiny and happy under her cowboy hat.

I can't talk because my brain is too excited imagining something huge. Maybe it's a new kind of dinosaur. Gram's been a paleontologist for forty years, but she's never discovered a new dinosaur.

"What is it?" Sam asks.

Gram slaps her knee. "It's an egg!"

A Dinosaur Egg
and a Weenie

I should probably explain that finding an egg fossil is really, really rare. I bet only one out of a gazillion people ever finds a dinosaur egg. You're more likely to get eaten by a shark *and* struck by lightning than find a dinosaur egg.

Sam and I climb into the back of Gram's brown truck. I think it used to be white, but it hasn't been washed in a long, long time.

"Wahoo!" Gram shouts as we speed up the dirt road. The new dig site is not on DECoW land. It's on the Crabtrees' cattle ranch.

I smile at Sam. She probably doesn't know this is the most exciting day of her life.

When we park, I'm the first one out of the truck. I race to the edge of the site. And there it is! The egg is the most beautiful thing I've ever seen. It's all black and kind of rough, not smooth like an egg from the fridge.

"If you ran that fast at soccer, maybe your team wouldn't lose all the time." I turn to see Aaron Crabtree chewing on a piece of grass. He's only eight, but he's bigger than two of me.

"We don't lose all the time," Sam says, putting her hands on her hips. "We were rained out once."

I don't care about soccer right now. There's a dinosaur egg sticking out of the ground right in front of me. It's the size of a football, and half of it is still buried in the limestone.

"It's not broken," I say.

"I know," Gram says, and her smile gets even bigger.

I super-careful walk into the pit, making sure not to step on any of the areas marked with white paint and a number. That's how we mark where the fossils are found.

Sam and Aaron jump into the pit.

"Be careful," one of the scientists grumbles. "Don't disturb the site." I'm glad he says it, so I don't have to.

"You're excited about a black rock?" Aaron asks.

Sam covers her microphone. "It's a dinosaur egg, you weenie."

"It's a perfect dinosaur egg," I add.

"This is my show, Frank." Sam holds up the microphone again. "Let's start from the top. In three, two, one. Gram, what kind of egg is it? A *T. rex*?"

"I don't know, Sam." Gram touches it with one finger. "It's not like any I've ever seen."

"If it's a brand-new dinosaur, what are you

going to name it?" Sam asks. "You should name it after your first grandchild. Me."

"No way," Aaron says. "This is my daddy's land. I'm naming this dinosaur egg, and I'm keeping it too."

"You want it? You have to get through me first!" I yell in Aaron's face. "And Sam. And my gram." My voice may sound brave, but my legs are shaking. I wish I wasn't wearing shorts.

"It looks like the two boys are about to start fighting," Sam says to her invisible camera. "Let's watch."

"There will be no fighting," Gram says. "The Crabtrees and the Mudds have an agreement. The Crabtrees can graze their cattle on our fields in the north. And all the fossils we find on Crabtree land will be displayed at the dinosaur center. You're welcome to come see them anytime, Aaron."

Good thing Gram broke us up because I was getting ready to run away. That would have been embarrassing. I'm not a fast runner.

Aaron rides off on his four-wheeler. Sam and I spend the rest of the day under the tent watching Gram and her scientists free the egg fossil.

I'm an expert-level fossil digger, but I'm not allowed out in the sun.

Around dinnertime, the egg is packed in a crate and loaded into the truck. Gram drives much slower back to the DECoW building.

I have a hard time falling asleep that night. Kind of like the time I ate three giant Pixy Stix at Jack Boyd's birthday party.

My brain finally turns off, and I close my eyes. I think I sleep for one minute before Saurus jumps on my head. I knock her off me, but she does it again.

"What, Saurus?"

She leaps off the bed and stands in front of the bedroom door.

I open it for her. She steps into the hallway and meows. She wants me to follow her. (Don't ask me how I know this. I just do.) We walk down the hall and past Sam's room. Her door is open a little bit. I peek inside.

"Where's Sam?" I ask.

Saurus keeps walking. We go down the stairs. Sam's not in the kitchen. Then I see a light outside. Someone is walking with a flashlight. It's Sam.

I watch her open the side door to DECoW.

"She's going to steal the egg," I say to Saurus. And—I swear this is true—Saurus nods yes.

I pull on my work boots and run out the front door. I think for a second that I should wake up Gram and PopPop. There's no time. I have to stop a thief!

Saurus jumps in her catmobile and we zoom across the parking lot. When we get inside the building, I tiptoe into the lab. The egg is still safe in its crate. Sam is standing in front of it. I can only see her back. Maybe she just came to look at it. Or interview it with her fake microphone.

Then I see Sam lift her arm. She has a hammer in her hand.

Born an Expert

"**N**o!" I scream.

Sam jumps.

"Don't hurt the egg!" I run across the lab and pull the hammer out of her hand.

"I just wanted to see what's inside," Sam says.

Sam hardly knows anything about dinosaurs or fossils or dinosaur fossils.

"There's probably nothing inside of it except

dirt that's turned to rock over the last sixty-five million years. No dinosaur bones. Once, I saw a dinosaur egg in a museum, and it did have fossilized bones inside. That's super rare, like winning a prize at the claw game."

She touches it. "It feels like a rock," she says, sounding disappointed.

"It's still amazing," I say. "Think about it. At one time, this egg held a baby dinosaur. No one has ever held a baby dinosaur."

"I bet he was a small dinosaur." Sam rubs the egg like it's a crystal ball.

"Maybe not. The biggest dinosaur egg ever found was only twenty-one inches long." I really should give Sam a class on dinosaurs.

Sam glares at me. "You think you know everything."

"I know a lot about dinosaurs. I was pretty much born an expert." This is true. My first book was an ABC dinosaur book. My first blanket had dinosaurs on it. My first stuffed animal was an *Iguanodon*.

"So you probably aren't going to let me crack this open, right?" Sam asks.

"Right."

"Then I'm going to bed." Sam rolls her eyes and leaves.

I put the hammer away.

"Come on, Saurus. Let's go." But Saurus doesn't get back in her catmobile. Instead, she jumps up and sits on the egg.

Do NOT sit on DINO EGGS!

"Get down or Gram is going to be so mad."
I pick up my cat. I look back at the egg. No
damage.

But then suddenly it twitches.

I rub my eyes and pinch myself to make sure
that I'm not sleeping. Then I pinch Saurus, and
she hisses. We are both definitely awake.

"Go get Gram," I whisper to Saurus. But she
doesn't.

The egg jumps and shakes for a minute. Then
it stops.

"What should we do?" I ask Saurus.

Saurus doesn't answer, but somehow I know
what she's thinking. She wants me to sit on the
egg.

"If something goes wrong, this is all your
fault."

So I sit on it. Only because I don't have a
choice. There are no living mommy dinosaurs

around to do it. Plus, I don't think I'm breaking any rules. Not really.

"This is crazy." Soon the egg is hopping again. It must like the feel of my butt. I stay on for a long time. Like three or four minutes.

CRACK!

You Won't Believe This (But It's True!)

I jump off the egg.

The first crack appears on the tip. I move the egg onto a lab table. My forehead sweats because I'm excited. (And a teeny-tiny bit scared out of my brain.) What if it's a dangerous raptor breaking free from its shell?

I step back.

More cracks grow. A piece of the shell falls off. This is soooo much better than a plastic

Easter egg. (And once, I even found a golden egg with a dollar inside it.)

Then a slimy head pushes through the shell. Its nose holes wiggle. It looks like an alligator but with a bump on the end of its snout. It's so cute . . . for a slimy blue-green thingy.

"Don't stop now," I whisper.

The little critter lets out a tiny cry that sounds like a balloon with a hole in it. Then it pushes and pushes, trying to break free from its egg.

Finally, the creature rolls out of the shell, leaving a gooey trail on the table. It stands up on two legs. It stares at me and then opens its mouth—a mouth full of tiny teeth.

It's definitely a dinosaur! (A boy dinosaur—I think.)

A million ideas mix up in my brain. Tell Gram. Don't tell Gram. Pick him up. Don't touch him. He needs food. He might eat me.

"Hi." I wave. "I'm Frank. And this is Saurus. Welcome to the Dinosaur Education Center of Wyoming." I really didn't know what else to say.

Saurus is much braver than I am. She walks right up to the dinosaur even though they are about the same size. And she licks him on the tip of his peanut-shaped horn.

"You aren't going to eat me, are you?" I whisper. "You probably think I'm your dad or something."

He lets me pick him up. He weighs about as

much as Saurus. I put him in the sink and turn on the water. He shivers.

He's ugly and awesome at the same time. He's also the biggest scientific discovery ever.

And I know exactly what I need to do next.

Time to start writing down everything. This might sound like homework, but it's all part of being a scientist. Good reports are really important if you want to win awards like Best Scientist of the Year.

I put my dinosaur on the lab's scale. I use a yardstick to measure his height. Then I write down what I know about him in an official DECoW notebook.

Birthday: July 7 at 11:00 p.m.
Species: Unknown
Weight: 9 pounds
Height: About 12 inches (He moves around
    too much to tell for sure.)

Looks: Has a peanut-shaped horn and walks
   on four legs
Other information: Likes to chew on my pen

"Don't eat that. I'll get you some real food. After we clean up."

I wash the goo off the table. Then I try to put the egg back together. I'm not really good at puzzles.

"Let's get you some dinner. Newborn animals need to eat." I put the dinosaur in the catmobile. Saurus hisses. "You can walk to the house this one time," I tell her.

When we get to the kitchen, I open the fridge and hold up the dinosaur so he can see what we have to eat.

The dinosaur's teeth are not razor sharp like a shark's or a tiger's. So I guess he's an herbivore (that means a plant-eater).

Gram has carrots and lettuce and tomatoes

and onions. We pick a carrot stick. Then I put the dinosaur and the carrot on the kitchen table.

The little guy tilts his head. He looks at the carrot. Then he looks at me.

"You eat it. See?" I take a bite off the end. "They taste better with ranch dressing."

I hold out the carrot for the dinosaur. He tries to bite the end. It's too hard. So I decide to be like a mama bird. I chew up the carrot and spit it on the table. He sniffs it for a second, and then he eats it all up. This is a little gross. It's also a lot awesome.

"Are you still hungry?" I get some lettuce from the fridge. I don't like lettuce. So I search the junk drawer for scissors but find a hole punch instead. I use it to make lettuce sprinkles. It works.

"You need a name." I don't want to give him a human name like Brent or Colin. I had three Colins in my class last year. It got really

confusing. I could name him Real Life Awesome Dinosaur. Too long. I stare at his horn.

"Peanut," I say. "That's a good name."

He lifts his head and blinks twice. I think he likes it.

The clock on the microwave says it's one a.m.

I really should wake up Gram and PopPop and tell them my big news.

But if I tell them now, Gram probably won't let Peanut sleep in my room. She's really good at making up new rules super-fast. No eating pickles on the couch. No spitting watermelon seeds at your cousin. No lassoes in the house. (All those rules were made just for Sam.)

I decide I'll tell Gram in the morning. It would be rude to wake her up in the middle of the night when it's not an emergency.

Before I crawl into bed, I write down more important stuff.

Name: Peanut
First meal: Chewed-up carrots and lettuce
    sprinkles
Other information: Likes to sleep in the
    middle of the bed

Little Dino Cutie

A super-loud "Ahhhhhhhhh!" knocks me out of bed. I put my hands over my ears and open my eyes. Sam is standing in my doorway and screaming like she just saw a two-headed monster.

But there's no monster. Only a baby dinosaur.

Peanut tumbles off my bed and scrambles under the dresser.

"Quiet!" I yell at Sam. "And close the door."
I crawl after Peanut.

"What was *that*?" Sam points with her microphone.

"It's a dinosaur. Duh." I put my head on the floor. My dinosaur is shaking.

"I knew it. I knew there was something cool in that egg." Sam gets down on her hands and knees and looks under the dresser.

I ignore her and talk to Peanut. "It's okay, Peanut. She's loud and sometimes mean, but she's family. She won't hurt you. Probably."

Peanut is curled up against the wall. I grab his front foot and gently pull him out.

"We're going to be famous," Sam says.

"I thought you were already famous," I remind her. Peanut snuggles against my shirt.

"Well, you'll be a little bit famous, and I'll be more famous." She moves closer, looking at

Peanut with one eyebrow raised. "What kind of dinosaur is he?"

"I don't know. He might be new."

"Can I hold him?" Sam asks. It's weird because she usually just tells me what to do.

"I guess."

Sam pats her lap. Peanut jumps for her.

"Oh, aren't you a good boy? Such a sweet dino. I love you already. Little dino cutie. Give me some kissie-kissies."

"Hey, cut it out. Don't baby-talk him. I'm trying to raise a big, tough dinosaur here. You're talking to him like he's a kitten." I look at Saurus. "No offense."

"I think he likes the baby-waby talk." Sam kisses his horn a thousand times.

"No." I pull Peanut away. "Where's Gram? I want to show her Peanut."

"That's not a good idea. Once I found a baby bunny, and Gram wouldn't let me keep it. She made me put it back in the fields." Sam shakes her head. "I bet she'll make you put Peanut out in a field. She'll say dinosaurs aren't meant to live in a house."

GRAM'S RULES
1. No Bunnies
2. No Dinosaurs

I let Sam hold him again while I change my clothes in the bathroom.

When I get back to the room, Sam has her microphone. "This is Sam McCarthy, and I'm here with the world's only real living dinosaur. His name is Peanut, and he's a *Samanthasaurus*."

"He is not a *Samanthasaurus*," I interrupt.

"Too late. I've already told the world." Sam smiles.

"You told an invisible camera." I shake my head. "And we should tell Gram and PopPop first."

"You're going to be sorry," Sam says. For some reason, I start to believe her.

Peanut wants to eat before he meets his great-grandparents. I know this because he keeps chewing on my thumb.

Saurus eats a can of smelly cat food. Peanut attacks a tomato. Sam and I have a bowl of no-sugar-added cereal. (Sam goes crazy if she has sugar.)

I should have told Gram and PopPop last night. I know Gram will be excited and happy. She might get kind of dizzy too. Just like me at my first Future Paleontologists meeting.

When we finish, we walk across the parking lot to the DECoW building. We make Peanut ride in my backpack. He squirms and claws to get out. But we don't want anyone to see him before we show Gram and PopPop. And Saurus refuses to share her catmobile.

There's a truck from the Crabtree cattle ranch parked out front.

"This can't be good," I whisper.

We leave the catmobile outside and sneak in through the side door. My stomach feels mushy and my forehead is sweaty. As soon as we get inside, we hear yelling.

"Uh-oh." Sam pulls out her microphone. "This sounds serious."

We creep up behind the gift-shop counter.

Gram is talking loudly. "We had an agreement, Mr. Crabtree. What kind of man goes back on his word?"

"Dr. Mudd, we shook hands. You have nothing in writing," Mr. Crabtree snaps. "You crazy scientist."

Sam jumps up. I pull her back down.

"Stay," I whisper. Sometimes I wish I had a dog instead of a cousin.

"Enough!" It sounds like PopPop, only scarier. "We had a deal. We let you graze your cattle on our land, and we're allowed to keep any fossils found at the site."

"That was before I knew what an egg fossil could be worth," Mr. Crabtree replies. "I'm done being a good neighbor. This is all business. I found a little museum in England willing to pay big money for that egg."

Gram and PopPop are quiet. I wish they would say something. Tell Mr. Crabtree to go climb a tree. (PopPop says that all the time to Sam.)

I peek over the counter. Gram shakes her head. PopPop puts a hand on her shoulder.

"We are not giving you the egg," PopPop says.

Mr. Crabtree taps his fingers

on the counter just above me. My heart freezes. I wish Peanut would freeze. He's twisting and turning so much it's like he's in a dryer.

"No," Gram says. "He can have the egg. We don't need to fight with our neighbors. It's not who we are."

"You're a wise woman, Dr. Mudd," Mr. Crabtree finally says. "Now get me my egg."

The Wicked West Dig Site
Lives Up to Its Name

Sam yanks my arm, and we speed out the side door before anyone can see us.

"What did you do with the egg?" she asks.

"It's still in the crate. Just in pieces. Lots of pieces."

"Okay." Sam walks back and forth. "Here's the plan. I'm going to go tell them I broke the egg. Everyone will believe that."

I nod. Sam has broken a lot of stuff since she got here.

"Then nobody will know it hatched," Sam says. "I'll tell them I used a hammer."

"That might work."

"I'll meet you somewhere out there." She points to the fields around DECoW.

"Let's go to the Wicked West site," I tell Sam. It's the site farthest to the west, and no one has done any digging there in three or four years.

"Good. Then we'll come up with a plan, but you need to get Peanut far away. Now." She gives me a little push.

Saurus is asleep in her catmobile, so I leave her behind. I think about maybe writing her a note, but I'm pretty sure she can't read. I get my bike and ride on the bumpy dirt road.

I was right. The site is empty. When I let

Peanut out of my backpack, he looks around at the rocks and bushes and dirt.

"Maybe now would be a good time to go to the bathroom," I say. He already made a few puddles and one pile in the house this morning. "And be careful of rattlesnakes."

Peanut goes from bush to rock to bush to rock. He sniffs everything.

"Just don't go over there." I point to the Crabtrees' land on the other side of the fence.

Either Peanut doesn't understand me or he doesn't like my rules. He runs right for the fence and easily sneaks under it.

"Peanut!" I run up to the fence. I can fit under it too, just not as quickly. I get down on my belly and squirm like a snake.

I chase him farther onto Crabtree land.

"Stop! Please!" I grab him right before he tries to crawl into a prairie dog hole.

"Don't you ever run away from me again."

I wag a finger at him, but he just tries to catch it with his mouth.

I start to relax and walk back. Then I hear the rumble of a four-wheeler coming our way.

I can't outrun it, and there's no good place to hide Peanut. I left my backpack over by the dig site. So I shove him in my shirt. It looks like I ate a soccer ball.

"Uggghhh." I only have one other idea. I pull off my shirt and wrap Peanut like a present. "Just stay still for a minute. Please."

The four-wheeler gets closer. The driver is wearing a helmet, but I know it's Aaron Crabtree.

He skids to a stop in front of me. Dirt flies in my face.

"What are you doing?" he asks as he takes off his goggles and helmet.

"Nothing," I say.

"This is Crabtree land," he says. "I could charge you rent. And I think I will. You owe me a quarter."

"I'm not staying." I try to walk past him.

"Doesn't matter," Aaron says.

"I don't have any money," I say. "I need to go get some."

"Maybe you got something to trade? What's in there?" He points at my shirt. I'm carrying it like a baby.

"It's my cat," I say. I'm kind of proud that I came up with a lie so quickly.

"Isn't *that* your cat?" Aaron points to the other side of the barbed-wire fence. I can't believe it. Saurus walked all the way out here on her own legs.

"Um ... I have, like, nine cats," I say. "Back home the kids at school call me the crazy cat boy."

Aaron nods like this all makes sense. "What happened to this one?"

"Bit by a rattlesnake, I think," I say.

"That's serious," Aaron says. "Quick, get on the four-wheeler. I'll drive you to my dad. He'll know what to do."

Why didn't I just say he was sleeping?

"No thanks," I say. "It was just a little snake. Worm-sized. He'll be okay." I walk around the four-wheeler.

"Do you wanna come over to my house and

throw rocks at stuff?" I think he's smiling and trying to be nice. Or maybe his teeth are stuck together and he wants to throw rocks at me.

"No thanks."

"I won't even charge you rent," Aaron says.

"No. I got important stuff to do. I have to wash my cats. All nine of them."

"Whatever." He puts his helmet back on. "I'll see you tomorrow at the soccer game. Get ready to lose."

"I was born ready." Wait, that didn't come out right.

Mushy Bananas with Worms

I **stay at the** Wicked West site for over an hour. Sam never comes. Maybe Gram and PopPop are so mad about the broken egg that they sent her home to California. Saurus spends the time licking her back legs. Peanut digs and jumps and gets very dusty-dirty.

It's hot out, and I'm thirsty. I put Peanut in my backpack and Saurus in my basket. Then I jump on my bike. Peanut doesn't like being treated like a binder. He chews at the zipper for a while. Right before I get to Gram and PopPop's, he finally stops wiggling and starts snoring.

I'm surprised when I see my grandparents sitting at the kitchen table. In the middle of the day, Gram and PopPop are usually out working. I stop in my tracks, and Peanut squirms in my backpack.

"Frank," Gram says when she sees me. "Where have you been?"

"I went for a bike ride." Not a lie.

PopPop looks at me kind of funny. I don't usually ride my bike just for fun.

"Where's Sam?" I ask.

"She's in her room," Gram answers. "She's grounded. Did you know she broke the egg fossil?"

I make my best surprised face. "No!"

"Mr. Crabtree was very upset," PopPop says with a little laugh. "Doesn't matter. There were no fossilized bones in the shell. Nothing was lost."

"Did you think there would be?" I ask.

"No, not really. But I was hoping." Gram smiles. "That would be a dream come true."

"Gram, do you ever wish you could find a real live dinosaur?" That seems like an even bigger dream.

"I can't say I ever really thought about it," she says.

"That would be something," PopPop says. "For almost two hundred years, scientists have been guessing what dinosaurs look like and how they acted. If we had a real dino, we could answer all these questions we have about them."

Gram lets out a puff of air. "Well, dear... if we had a dinosaur, we would learn a lot about its color and size. But we wouldn't learn how it behaves in a pack or how it hunts or feeds in the wild. I think it would be a very sad dinosaur."

"Or maybe not," I say.

"It would be kept in a pen and watched all the time," Gram says.

"Would it get shots?" I hate shots. I'd rather eat mushy bananas with worms than get a shot. When I told the doctor that, she said mushy bananas with worms didn't have the same disease-fighting powers.

"Lots of shots, I bet." Gram shakes her head. "That's why I study extinct animals. I don't have to worry about hurting them."

I take a deep breath. I'll never let anyone hurt Peanut. And neither will Gram.

"I need to tell you something," I say.

Before I can say another word, Sam bursts into the kitchen.

"Stop everything!" she shouts.

"What's wrong?" PopPop asks.

"Frank!" Sam screams even though she's only two feet away from me. "I need to talk to you. It's important. And urgent. And top-secret."

Sam's yelling is making Peanut nervous. He twists and turns in my backpack. This makes me nervous, so I start twisting and turning.

"Frank, why are you dancing?" PopPop asks.

"He's not dancing. I think he's got fleas." Sam yanks my arm and drags me up the stairs.

"But Frank wanted to tell us something," Gram calls from behind me.

When we get to my bedroom, I put my backpack on the floor. Peanut jumps out as soon as I unzip it.

"Were you going to tell Gram and PopPop without me?" Sam asks.

"They love dinosaurs. It'll be okay."

"No. It. Won't." Sam grabs the front of my shirt. "If the Crabtrees find out, they will take him."

I shake my head. "Gram would never let them."

"You weren't there," Sam says. "After I got an epic lecture about breaking the egg, Mr. Crabtree forced Gram to sign a contract. Everything from that dig site belongs to him. Everything!"

"So what are we going to do?" I pick up Peanut.

"I don't know, but we have to keep him a secret. It shouldn't be too hard. He's small."

"For now," I say. Peanut could grow to be as big as a dog . . . or bigger than three elephants.

"We'll hide him. Then at the end of the summer, I'll take him home to California. Everybody has weird pets in California. Our neighbor has a hairless cat. It has the biggest ears you've ever seen."

"You can't keep him. He'll go home with me."
Mom's allergic to dogs, but I don't think she's
allergic to dinosaurs.

"If he comes to California with me, he can
be a movie star," Sam says. She pulls her plastic microphone out of
her back pocket and
holds it toward Pea-
nut. "See, he wants
to be famous."

"No, he wants to
eat again."

"He can eat in
a minute. First, it's
picture time." Before
I can stop her, Sam runs to get her camera.

"No pictures," I say. "He's supposed to be a
secret, remember?" I try to grab the camera. She
hides it behind her back.

"But you're writing down all this stuff about him," Sam says. "What are your notes for?"

"That's for science, not for fun." Though it *is* fun.

"Well, my pictures are for science too. And my friends at home." She smiles. "Just kidding."

"We have another problem. What are we going to do with him during the soccer game tomorrow?"

Sam shrugs. "I guess Saurus could babysit?"

It's not a great idea, but it's the only one we come up with. The next morning, we lock Peanut and Saurus in my room.

"I'm sure they'll be good," Sam says. "What could go wrong?"

The Dino Needs a Time-Out

"**I can't believe** I scored five goals," Sam says. "That's got to be a record."

"Four were for the other team," I remind her. "Aaron Crabtree's team." We walk down the hallway toward our bedrooms.

"It's really quiet," Sam says. "That's a good sign." She pushes open the door.

A tornado named Peanut has hit my room.

There's a hole in the bed. The blankets are

shredded. He has knocked everything off of everything. He has chewed the furniture.

Peanut is asleep in the middle of a pile of clothes. Destroying an entire room must be tiring. I grab something orange. It's a sleeve without the rest of the shirt.

"What a disaster," Sam says. "I'm glad we didn't leave him in my room."

"Your room always looks like this." Then my heart gets really fast. *Where's my cat?*

"Saurus!" I yell.

Meow. The sound comes from above my head. Saurus is lying on the curtain rod.

"How did she get up there?" Sam asks.

I drag a chair over so I can reach her.

"Help me clean up," I say to Sam.

"I think a bulldozer would be faster," she says, and then leaves. I clean for a while. Peanut sleeps the whole time. That is a good thing because he's going to get a long lecture when he wakes up.

I get tired of picking up pieces of stuff and trying to put them back together. So I just shove everything in the closet. It goes much faster this way.

Peanut wakes up. I'm ready with my lecture. I'm even thinking he might need a time-out. But then he sees me, and he's so excited that his whole body shakes.

I bend down, and he jumps into my arms.

"I missed you too," I say as Peanut licks my face. Peanut is either asleep or full of energy. He doesn't do anything in between.

• • •

The next days are a lot of work. Turns out watching a baby dinosaur is a full-time job. And another job that I don't get paid for.

We try to teach him to use a litter box.

It didn't work, so Sam tries to make him a diaper. He chews it off.

I try to get him to walk on a leash. When the leash is on, he lies down. When the leash is off, he runs away.

3. WASHING (No bubble bath)

4. Teaching Tricks

Sam tries to give him a bath. Peanut ends up eating a lot of bubbles.

Sam also tries to teach him tricks. She still thinks they will be on TV. I'll never let that happen.

I try to teach him to sleep on the end of the bed. But he likes the middle. Sometimes I just give up and sleep on the floor.

And I know Gram is onto us. I haven't worked

at DECoW in five days. Last night she said, "I hardly see you anymore. You and Sam must be having lots of fun."

I explain all of this to Sam in the backyard. I need to get back to work.

"Just tell Gram you're sick," Sam suggests. "Chicken pox or the flu. You could have caught it from him." She points at Peanut, who's digging in an old sandbox.

"Dinosaurs didn't have the flu or chickens." I repin my name tag so that it's on straight.

"How do you know? Maybe that's what made them go extinct." Sam sits on the only swing that isn't broken.

"Just keep Peanut safe," I say. "I'm gonna help Gram clean fossils until lunchtime. Can you be responsible?"

"Yes, sir." Sam salutes me.

I hand her a list of rules, and she makes a sputter noise. I guess maybe I shouldn't be so

worried about Peanut. I mean, his egg did sur-
vive for 65 million years. He's pretty tough.

I put Saurus in her catmobile, and we cross
the parking lot to work. For two hours, I try to
clean the jaw fossil in front of me. I dip a tooth-
brush in water and gently brush away the stone
around the fossil. But it's hard to focus. I keep
thinking of Peanut.

I accidentally knock over my water. "Ugghh."

"Are you all right?" Gram asks. She's working
on a larger fossil.

I wonder what Sam and Peanut are doing.

"I don't feel good." I put my hand on my forehead. "I think I have dino pox. Um . . . I mean,
chicken pox."

"Is that so?" Gram says. "I hear you can cure
dino pox by playing with your cousin."

"Really? Okay." I yank off my lab coat and
throw it on the hook. "See you later, Gram." I
run outside to the swing set. They're not there.

I go inside the house.

"Sam!" I yell as I check each room. It's all quiet.

She must have taken him for a bike ride. Even though that would break rule number twenty-seven. *Stay close to the house.*

I go into the garage. Both bikes are there.

Suddenly my stomach feels gushy, but this is not the time to puke. I go back to the dinosaur center. PopPop's working the front desk.

"Hi, PopPop. Have you seen Sam?" My voice is jumpy and I don't sound like myself.

"Not since breakfast." He takes off his glasses.

I'm about to tell him everything because I don't like being worried alone. But then I see Sam walking across the parking lot. She's holding Peanut in her arms, all out in the open where anyone could see him.

"Gotta go."

We've Been Spied On

When I **meet** them in our driveway, Peanut is shaky and Sam's nose is sniffly.

"What's wrong?" I grab Peanut and look at him top, sides, and bottom. He's not hurt.

"We went for a walk and Aaron Crabtree saw us!" Sam

uses the back of her hand to wipe away snot. "He was spying."

"Where were you?" I ask.

Sam shrugs.

"Sam?"

"At the soccer field," Sam whispers. I don't think I've heard her whisper before.

I want to yell at Sam. She didn't follow the rules again. And I trusted her.

"What do we do?" Sam asks.

"We need to tell Gram. He's not a secret now." I pat the top of his head. My stomach hurts knowing he's not just mine (and a little bit Sam's) anymore.

Sam nods. "Okay."

The parking lot of DECoW is more crowded than most days.

"We can't take him into the center. There are too many people." I hand Peanut to Sam. "Bring him to the house. I'll go get Gram and PopPop."

Peanut snuggles against Sam's neck. It's like he's trying to figure out why she's sad.

PopPop is busy at the front desk selling tickets to the museum. He waves at me as I rush by.

"Looks like you found your cousin. Is everything all right?" he asks.

I don't stop to answer his question. I just nod a lot.

Gram is still cleaning fossils, but she's not alone. A family with two little boys is there too. For twenty dollars anyone can clean fossils.

"Gram." I tug on the sleeve of her lab coat. She's busy trying to keep the littlest boy from brushing on his fossil too hard.

"One minute, Frank." She doesn't even look at me.

"It's kinda, sorta an emergency."

The mom, who has been taking pictures, stops and stares at me.

"Is it kinda, sorta an emergency? Or is it an

emergency?" This time Gram does look at me. I wonder if the answer might be written on my face.

"No one is hurt or anything. Nothing's on fire or flooded or bleeding. But it's important."

"All right," Gram says. "Let me find someone to assist this nice family."

It feels like forever before I finally get Gram away from them. Now we need to get PopPop.

When we get to the front desk, PopPop is still behind the counter and Sam is sitting next to him eating a granola bar.

"Where's Peanut?" I scream-ask.

"Peanut?" Gram asks.

Sam wrinkles her eyebrows. "He's sleeping in your room. You were gone a long time. I came to find you."

"You left Peanut alone?" I don't wait for an answer. I run out of DECoW and toward the house.

"Who's Peanut?" Gram asks. She and Sam are right behind me.

The front door is open. My hands are sweaty and the hairs on my arms tingle. I dart up the stairs two at a time, something I've never done before.

"Peanut?" I call out.

My room is a disaster. Again. But this time I get the feeling it wasn't Peanut.

I get down on my hands and knees and look under the bed, the dresser, the desk, and even the rug. No dinosaur.

"Frank Louis Mudd, what happened in here?" Gram is in the doorway. So is Sam.

"It didn't look like this ten minutes ago," Sam says. "I promise. I left him sleeping on your bed."

I get in Sam's face. "And you left the door open."

"No, I didn't. I promise. I remember closing it real soft so I wouldn't wake him up." Sam crosses her heart with a finger.

"He's gone!" I try to run past Gram, but she grabs my arm.

"What's going on?" she asks.

"There's no time to explain. Our dinosaur is missing," I answer.

But it turns out, there is time to explain. Gram makes me. We all go to the kitchen, and Sam and I confess everything.

Gram and PopPop don't say anything while we talk. Gram's mouth hangs open, and Pop-Pop's eyebrows go up.

"Now he's run away," Sam says.

"No. I bet Aaron Crabtree took him," I add. "And we have to get him back."

Sending Out a Search Party

I can tell PopPop and Gram don't believe us. They do that adult thing where they nod a lot, but it doesn't mean yes.

"You're very creative children," PopPop says, smiling.

"I've got proof," Sam says. She darts out of the room and comes back with her camera. She shows Gram the screen.

Gram tilts her head.

She shows PopPop.

He squints.

Then she shows me.

"I thought we said no pictures. That was one of the rules." I look at the camera. Sam isn't a very good photographer. The blue-green blob on the screen could be Peanut or a smashed pickle with a horn.

"You have too many rules. And it was good that I broke your silly rule. We can use the picture on our missing dinosaur poster." Sam smirks and puts a hand on her hip.

"And if you'd followed my other rules, he wouldn't be missing." I push my finger in her face.

Gram takes the camera again. She holds the picture a few inches from her nose. "That's the dinosaur?"

"Yes, we need to find him," Sam says.

"Let's split up," I suggest.

Gram and PopPop look at each other for a long time. Then PopPop shrugs, which means they will help us search.

PopPop and Sam head outside and start searching around the house and the fields and DECoW. Gram and I get into her truck and head to the Crabtrees' ranch.

She mumbles under her breath as she drives. I can't understand her. But that's okay because I don't think she's really talking to me.

We ride up the longest driveway in the world. Gram stops the truck in front of the house.

Three big dogs run off the porch. They are barking like crazy.

If Peanut is here, he's probably scared. He's never met a dog before.

A lady steps out of the house. She's wearing overalls and holding a paintbrush.

"Hi, Rebecca." Gram waves as we get out of the truck.

"Morning, Susan," the woman calls. "Are you looking for Harry?"

"No, we're looking for Aaron," Gram says.

"Come on in." Mrs. Crabtree holds the door open. "Has he done something?"

Gram plays with her truck keys. I've never seen Gram look nervous before, so I decide to help her out.

"He kidnapped my dinosaur!" I blurt out. "And I want him back."

Mrs. Crabtree gives me a worried smile. "I don't understand. Let me get Aaron." She leaves us standing by the front door. I look around the living room for evidence of a dinosaur. Nothing.

"Maybe you should let me handle this," Gram says.

"Well," Mrs. Crabtree says, "I'm sorry, but he's not in his room. Are you saying he stole your toy?" She scratches her head with the end of the paintbrush.

"It's hard to explain," Gram says. "When you see him, can you, um ... let him know that I need to speak with him?"

"Of course," Mrs. Crabtree says. She opens the front door, and we head back to the truck. The dogs bark again but don't get too close.

I give them my best evil eye. "Don't you hurt my dinosaur," I whisper, because dogs have really good hearing and Gram doesn't.

Mrs. Crabtree calls during dinner. She tells Gram that Aaron doesn't know anything about a missing toy dinosaur. She says he spent the day working in the barn. I call Mrs. Crabtree a liar (not to her face), and Gram makes me sit on a stool in the corner and think about it for ten minutes.

After dinner, Sam and I are allowed to go outside and search some more. We promise three things. To stay together. To keep close to the house. To be back inside before dark.

We find nothing.

Gram tucks me into bed. I don't want to go to bed because I know I'm never going to fall asleep. Peanut is still missing and so is Saurus. No one has seen my cat since this morning. We found her catmobile still parked in the museum.

This is the worst day of my life.

I lie in my bed and stare at the ceiling. After a while, there's a knock on my door.

"Come in."

It's Sam. She's holding her pillow and a fuzzy blanket.

"Can I sleep in here?" she asks.

"Sure, but I can't sleep."

Sam makes her bed on the floor, and we both stare at the ceiling.

"I'm sorry, Frank," Sam says. "I should have watched him better." She sniffs, and I don't remember her having a cold.

"It's not your fault. I should have told Gram right away. I was being selfish," I say.

"Yeah," Sam says. "You kinda were."

I only shake my head because I'm too tired to argue. The room is quiet, which is my least favorite sound. My stomach growls because I didn't eat much dinner. I was too worried.

Then I hear a tap and a ping.

"What was that?" Sam asks.

The noise came from outside. I get to the

window a second before Sam does. Aaron Crabtree is throwing pebbles at my room. I open the
window.

"Where's my dinosaur?" I yell.

"He's at my house." Aaron's voice shakes. "I
think he's sick."

Zombies, Vampires, and Dinos

Sam and I get on our bikes and follow Aaron.

I have a million questions bouncing in my brain, but there's no time. I just pedal fast and try to keep up.

Aaron skids to a stop outside a shed and lets his bike fall to the ground. The shed doesn't have any windows, but I can see light sneaking out of the cracks. Aaron pushes the sliding door open.

I see Saurus first. She's sitting up. She looks at us and lets out a sad meow. Then I see she's sitting next to a blue-green lump.

I shove past Aaron. Peanut is curled up on a baseball jacket. He's not moving.

"Peanut!" I call. He still doesn't move.

"Is he dead?" Sam asks.

"No," Aaron answers.

I get on my knees and put my hand softly on his back. He feels hot and sticky wet. His eyes open and I give him a big smile. He lifts his head a little, and then he goes back to sleep.

I turn to Aaron, who is standing behind me. "What did you do?"

"Nothing." He rocks back and forth. "We had an awesome time. I took him horseback riding. We had a water-gun fight. I fed him gummy worms and double-chocolate cookies."

"What?" I stand up so fast, Saurus jumps out of my way. "You can't feed a dinosaur junk food!" This all needs to be written down in my notebook, just not right now.

"How would I know what you're supposed to feed a dinosaur? I know you feed brains to a zombie and blood to a vampire. But dinosaurs aren't real."

"You shouldn't have taken him!" I give him a little push.

"Stop!" Sam yells. "Look."

Peanut is shaking. When he finally stops, he moans. Saurus steps in and licks Peanut's horn.

I'm afraid if we pick him up, we'll hurt him. "He needs a doctor."

"Let's take him to Gram," Sam says.

"Your grandma isn't a doctor," Aaron says.

"Yeah, she is!" Sam says. "It's part of her name. Dr. Susan Mudd. Dinosaur expert." Sam leans in. "She knows everything about dinosaurs, *and* she makes the best French toast."

"My daddy takes care of hundreds of cattle every day. He even helps them be born," Aaron says.

"Get them both!" I yell. "Just hurry."

For a second, Aaron and Sam look at each other. Then the race is on. The bikes fly down the driveway. Sam is a lot faster, but Mr. Crabtree is a lot closer.

I sit down on the wooden floor. Saurus keeps watch with me.

"Have you been with him the whole time?" I ask.

And I swear this is true, Saurus actually nods.

"You're a good cat." I rub her head.

Then I lean down and kiss Peanut on the horn. "Be strong, little guy. Help will be here soon."

I just hope I'm not lying.

Please Help My Terrible Lizard

Mr. Crabtree and Aaron are the first to arrive. Saurus hears them coming and hides.

"Holy smokes!" Mr. Crabtree booms. "Get away from it, boy." He pulls me back by the shoulders. "It's dangerous."

I wiggle out of his grasp. "He's not dangerous. He's a baby, and he's sick."

"This is from the egg?" Mr. Crabtree points at Peanut. "*My* egg."

"Dad, you have to help him," Aaron begs.

"What do I know about lizards?" Mr. Crabtree says. For a man who is bigger than a bear, he looks afraid of a nine-pound dinosaur.

"Actually," I say, "he's not a lizard. I know it's confusing because the word *dinosaur* means 'terrible lizard.' But he's a different kind of reptile."

"I don't know much about reptiles either, boy. I know cattle and horses."

Peanut lets out a small chirp and shudders. I sit on the ground and pull him gently into my lap. "Don't be scared."

We hear the truck rattling along the gravel driveway.

"Your grandparents are here," Aaron says from the doorway. "Maybe they'll know what to do."

Gram is in the door first. She marches over to me and takes my face in her hands, which is really embarrassing.

"Frank, are you . . . ?" Then Gram sees Peanut for the first time. Her eyebrows move so high on her forehead, I think they might fly off her face.

"This is Peanut, my dinosaur. He's sick."

She puts one hand on his chest and one shaky hand on his head. Peanut's eyes open.

"I can't believe this," Gram says.

PopPop comes into the shed too. It's getting crowded.

"That's not a ... It can't be." He pulls off his glasses and rubs his eyes.

"It is," Sam says.

"Great gumdrops. I never thought I'd see a real dinosaur," PopPop says.

"Can you help him?" I ask Gram.

"Please, Gram." Sam kneels down next to us.

"I don't know what to do for him," Gram says. "He needs a veterinarian."

"I've got a good vet," Mr. Crabtree says. "I'm sure he's never treated a dinosaur, but he worked at a zoo once. He's in Jackson Hole."

"That's two hours away," I say.

"Call him," Gram says.

Mr. Crabtree goes outside to use his cell phone.

"May I hold him?" Gram asks.

I nod and put Peanut into her arms.

When Mr. Crabtree's off the phone, he tells us that his friend has agreed to see Peanut.

"I don't know if he believed me, but he's willing to see us. Even in the middle of the night."

"Great, thank you, Mr. Crabtree." Gram smiles. "If you'll just give us his address, we'll get going."

Mr. Crabtree stands over us and blocks all the light. "I don't think so, Dr. Mudd. This is my dinosaur. I'll be taking him to the vet."

Gram and Mr. Crabtree talk at the same time. We are in the shed, but they are using outside voices to argue about Peanut.

"Stop it!" Aaron yells. "We can figure this all out later. He's sick, and it's my fault. You gotta help him."

"Just make him feel better," I add.

Mr. Crabtree grunts and squishes his lips together.

"Let's both take him," Gram says. "The kids are right. This is not the time."

"Let's all go," Sam says.

"No," both Gram and Mr. Crabtree answer.

There's no time to argue. The longer we talk, the longer it will take for Peanut to get to the vet.

Gram tells us to say goodbye. I don't want to.

Sam goes first. "It's not goodbye. It's see you later." She's thinking the same thing I am. We just have to see him again.

"Sorry, Zeke," Aaron says, rubbing Peanut's horn.

"That's not his name," Sam mumbles.

Then it's my turn. I really can't talk. My throat's all tight and scratchy. I give him a little squeeze. He knows I'll be waiting for him.

We watch from the Crabtrees' front porch as Gram, PopPop, and Mr. Crabtree leave in Gram's truck. Peanut sits on Gram's lap in the backseat.

"They'll call as soon as they know anything," Mrs. Crabtree says. "Come inside."

Sam and I share the couch, and Aaron sits in the chair. The TV is on, but no one's watching. Mrs. Crabtree makes us popcorn. No one eats. It's after midnight. No one's tired.

"If you had told me, I would have kept your secret," Aaron says.

"No offense, but I don't believe you," Sam says.

Aaron slumps in the chair, and I believe him, at least a little bit.

"Do you think he'll be okay?" I ask.

"Yeah. Of course." Sam likes to be positive. She thinks our team can win soccer games. She also thinks she's going to star in a Disney movie.

"If he is okay . . ." I rub my eyes. "Then what?"

Aaron only shrugs.

"You know my gram and your dad are going to keep fighting," I say.

"And Gram never backs down," Sam says. "She's the toughest person I know."

"My dad never loses. Not soccer games, not

go-fish, not anything." Aaron isn't really bragging. It sounds more like complaining.

"They'll keep arguing until either they go extinct or Peanut does," Sam adds.

I sit up and take a pad of paper and a pen off the coffee table. "Then it's up to us to figure something out."

Sam's stinky feet are in my face. I shove them off, and she tumbles off the couch.

"Hey!" she yells.

The sun shines through the Crabtrees' living room window.

"What time is it?" I wipe the drool off my cheek. We must have fallen asleep finally. We spent hours figuring out where Peanut would live. And his name. He's now officially Peanut Zeke McCarthy. (I picked the first name, Aaron

got the middle name, and McCarthy is Sam's last name.)

Aaron stretches on the floor. He yawns loud like a lion. "It's almost ten." He points to a clock on the fireplace mantel.

"Good morning," Mrs. Crabtree says. "Would anyone like some breakfast?" She smiles so big it looks painted on her face.

I stand up. "Has my gram called?"

"No, not yet. I'm sorry."

We all follow Mrs. Crabtree into the kitchen. She takes out a frying pan and makes us pancakes. Aaron helps, while Sam and I set the table. We just start to eat when the phone rings. I jump up to get it but stop because it's not my house.

Mrs. Crabtree answers it in the other room. I can't hear anything she's saying.

"We need to go to the animal hospital," she says when she returns.

"Is Peanut okay?" I ask.

"Your grandfather just said to come quickly."

And we do. We don't even clear the table, but Mrs. Crabtree makes us all use the bathroom first because it's a long drive.

Aaron, Sam, and I sit in the backseat. We are at the end of their driveway when I tell Mrs. Crabtree to stop.

"We have to bring Saurus. Saurus is like Peanut's mom," I say.

Mrs. Crabtree nods. When she pulls up in front of Gram and PopPop's house, Saurus is sitting by the front door. She knew we needed her.

The ride takes two hours, and no one talks. I grab Sam's hand. She grabs Aaron's. If Peanut is okay, we have a plan to keep him safe and in Wyoming.

PopPop is pacing in the parking lot of the animal hospital. There are lots of cars and people and pets.

"Is Peanut okay?" I ask as I jump out of the car.

"He's had a rough night," PopPop says. "This way. We need to go in through the back. And don't mention Peanut's, um . . . breed."

I turn and grab Saurus. She must be able to read because she definitely knows this is a vet's office, and she doesn't want to go in.

"Relax, we're not here for you," I say, and she settles down a little.

PopPop leads us inside, and we walk down a quiet hallway. The lights above hum.

"Here." PopPop opens a door.

My stomach drops.

On the table in the middle of the room is Peanut, and he's not moving.

The Plan

We rush over to Peanut. I smile when I see that he's breathing. Then I notice the colored tape on his arms and legs. They must have stuck him with a bunch of needles.

Gram comes up behind us. "The doctor took x-rays and used a tube to empty Peanut's stomach. He had to give Peanut some medicine to keep him asleep and still. We're waiting for him to wake up."

I let out a deep breath. Saurus wiggles out of my arms and onto the metal table. She walks around Peanut a few times and then lies down next to him.

"So he'll be okay?" Sam asks.

The man in a white lab coat smiles. "I've never treated a dinosaur before, but most animals recover from anesthesia quickly."

"Then we can take him home?" I ask.

Gram turns and looks at Mr. Crabtree. He's sitting in the corner drinking coffee.

Aaron steps in front of his father. "Um, Dad? We have a plan."

Mr. Crabtree only grunts.

"Listen to the kids," Mrs. Crabtree says. She knows our plan. She was spying from the kitchen when we came up with it. Most moms spy.

Sam pulls out her microphone and looks into her invisible camera. "This is Sam McCarthy reporting from some vet place in Wyoming.

Peanut, the world's only dinosaur, will live in Wyoming forever."

"You have a lot of land," Aaron says to his dad.

"And *you* have a lot of land," I say to Gram.

"You can each donate some space," Sam adds. "Then we'll build a big fence around it and maybe a house for him to live in. Like a dinosaur zoo, but we'll be the only visitors."

"When he's ready," I say, petting his head. "He's too small right now to move out of my bedroom."

"I raise cattle," Mr. Crabtree says. "I'm not looking to raise something that might eat my cattle."

"Don't worry, he's an herbivore. He doesn't like steak," I say.

"I think we can reach some kind of agreement," PopPop adds. "There's plenty of room for your cattle and one measly dinosaur."

Mr. Crabtree scratches his chin for a long time. "This could work. We can charge folks to see him. If people are willing to pay ten dollars to see bones at your dinosaur center, I bet they'd pay a hundred dollars to see a real one. We'll sell T-shirts and stuffed animals. For an extra fifty dollars, visitors can feed him."

"No," I say. "He's part of our family."

"Our herd," Sam says.

"Don't you see?" Mr. Crabtree points at Peanut. "This little fella is a gold mine."

"But he's also just a baby." Mrs. Crabtree rubs Peanut's back.

"For now, I suggest we keep him a secret," Gram says. "Until we have a permanent home for him and know more about him."

"That's one big secret, Dr. Mudd." Mr. Crabtree shakes his head.

"Yes, it is. We will have to share Peanut someday," Gram says. "He's too amazing to keep to ourselves."

"What?" I can't believe what Gram is saying.

"He doesn't belong to us," Gram explains. "And he doesn't belong to the Crabtrees. We will keep him safe, but someday we will have to share him with scientists and children and other people who love dinosaurs."

"Can someday be one hundred years from now?" I ask.

"No." Gram laughs, and then hugs me.

Mr. Crabtree grunts again. "Fine. We'll keep quiet for now. But in time he will need to earn his keep."

"Hey, he's waking up," Aaron says.

I bend down so we're eye to eye. "Hey, Peanut. Guess what? You're going to get a home of your very own."

I Promise

Today Peanut is two weeks old. He weighs fifteen pounds and spends most of his day eating leaves and grass, which I guess are vegetables.

Gram and I are keeping track of all this stuff together. I still use my notebook, and she uses a computer.

Today Peanut is also getting a bath because he likes to roll around in stuff. Stinky stuff.

I take him outside to a plastic kiddie pool in the backyard. Sam has filled it with water, and Aaron has brought over some chew toys. Once Peanut sees the pool, he takes off and dives in headfirst.

"He's one fast dinosaur," Aaron says. "You really should put him on your soccer team."

"Yeah." Sam laughs. "Except he'd chew up the ball and poop on the field."

I'm just glad there are only two soccer games left.

Peanut jumps out of the pool and runs around us. He shakes water all over Aaron, and then goes for Sam.

"No!" Sam shrieks when Peanut nudges her with his horn. She uses the hose to spray him in the butt.

Then he turns toward me.

"Gotta catch me first." I run behind the rusty swing set and up the slide. Peanut is too slippery. He slides back down. He looks sad, so I slide down and wrap my arms around his neck.

"I'll never leave you, Peanut. I promise."

After his bath, Peanut is ready for a nap. We take him inside to the living room. Sam made him a bed with old blankets and a laundry basket. He uses it during the day. At night, he still sleeps on my bed.

I lay him down. Aaron pats his back.

"Sleep tight, Peanut," Sam says.

Peanut closes his eyes. We tiptoe toward the door. We have to be quiet during dinosaur naptime.

But just as we are almost out of the room, Gram comes running into the house.

"Hot dog!" she yells. "You'll never guess what we found at the new dig site."

Peanut jumps up. So much for a nap. He will be cranky later.

"What?" Sam asks.

"Is it another egg?" I ask.

"Nope," Gram says. "Think bigger!"

The End (almost)

Reader,

So that's my story. The first part, anyway. Don't forget the promise you made in the beginning. Don't tell anyone what you've read. Not your best friend. Not your parents. Not your teacher. You can tell your cat (as long as your cat can't speak or write).

Maybe someday we will share Peanut with the world. But for now he's our secret. So shhhhhh.

Sincerely,
Frank Mudd

P.S. Remember, if you spill the beans, I'll deny EVERYTHING!

Now that we are at the back of the book, I want to add another About the Author:

The author of this epic book is Frank L. Mudd. He's still nine years old, still handsome, and still a dinosaur expert. He hopes to live at DECoW with his parents, his cat, his grandparents, and his dinosaur. His favorite cousin is Sam. His favorite sport is soccer—not really. His favorite neighbor is Aaron. Frank is very good at hatching dinosaurs, hatching plans, and following the rules (most of the time). Here's a picture of him:

Sam   Aaron   FRANK
       (Peanut)

Glossary

Here are some words and definitions in case you aren't a dinosaur expert like me.

carnivore: An animal that eats meat. They usually have sharp teeth.

dig site: An area where scientists (and their grandkids) can dig up fossils.

fossil: Parts of plants or animals preserved in rock. Kind of like a scrapbook made by nature.

Hadean Eon: When the earth was born, about 4.5 billion years ago.

hadrosaurid: A duck-billed dinosaur that ate plants.

herbivore: An animal that eats only plants. Herbivore dinosaurs outnumbered carnivore dinos. (They had to outrun them too.)

Mesozoic Era: When dinosaurs roamed the earth, about 250 million to 65 million years ago.

Microraptor: Small feathered dinosaur that might have been able to glide (but not fly).

paleontologist: A scientist that studies prehistoric life, like dinosaurs. (They study plants and stuff too, but I don't think that's as much fun.)

Spinosaurus: A meat-eating dinosaur that had a huge spine running down its back. It was bigger than a *T. rex*!

Supersaurus: A huge plant-eating dinosaur that roamed the USA before it was the USA.

Triceratops: Means three-horned face. This dino walked on all four legs, ate plants, and had a huge skull.

About the [other] Author

(also known as the boring part of the book)

Stacy McAnulty does not have a dinosaur. She does have three kids, two dogs, and one husband. She has been on a dinosaur dig in Wyoming, where she found a small fossil. It wasn't an egg. Stacy grew up in upstate New York but now calls North Carolina home. (She still really wants a dinosaur—preferably a *Spinosaurus*.) Visit her online at stacymcanulty.com.

About the Illustrator

Mike Boldt loves ice cream, comics, and drawing. He is the illustrator of *I Don't Want to Be a Frog* and the author and illustrator of the forthcoming *A Tiger Tail*. Mike lives in Alberta, Canada, only a couple of hours from Drumheller, the site of that country's largest collection of dinosaur fossils.

Can Frank and Sam hide Peanut when he gets bigger?

Turn the page for a sneak peek
of the next Dino Files book!

"It looks like the horn on Peanut's snout," Aaron whispers.

"Exactly like it," Sam says. "Except a thousand times bigger."

"Not a thousand times bigger." Gram laughs. "Maybe a hundred times."

Peanut's horn is smaller than my pinky finger. This horn is longer than all of me.

The dad walks around with his camera.

"This is amazing," he says. "Brent, you probably made the dinosaur discovery of the century."

Probably not the discovery of the century, I think.

I look over at the truck, where a real dinosaur is locked inside. The truck shakes and rattles like a huge beast is trying to escape. Peanut is only fifteen pounds. He better learn some rules before he is bigger than a house.

"Excuse me," the dad calls to Gram.

"Yes." Gram puts on a fake smile.

"What kind of dinosaur is it?" he asks.

Sam jumps in front of the camera. "It's a *Wyomingasaurus.*" Sam likes to jump in front of cameras. She thinks she's famous.

"Samantha." Gram gives her a warning look.

Sam talks into her plastic microphone. She

never goes anywhere without it. "This is Sam McCarthy signing out."

"My son discovered a *Wyomingasaurus*." The dad gives us a big thumbs-up. "Brent, go sit on the fossil."

"No!" Gram and I yell.

"It's very fragile," she explains.

We wait for the family to take a million more pictures. I wish they would hurry. Peanut is squealing in the truck. Finally, they pack up their stuff and drive away.

"That horn has been here for over sixty-five million years," Gram says when we go back to the house for dinner. "It will be here tomorrow too."

The minute we walk in the door, PopPop calls us into the kitchen.

"You're going to want to see this," he says.

The small TV on the counter is on. Sam pushes me out of the way to get a look.

We all stare at the screen. I'm too shocked to talk. But not Sam.

"I'm famous!" she shouts. "I'm finally famous."